IKEY,
The
Little Seashell

by
Sarah Walker Becton, M.A.

Co-authored and
Illustrated by
Daniel Walker Becton, Ph.D.

▲ BLUE NOTE BOOKS
F L O R I D A

First Edition

ISBN No. 1-878398-58-X

Library of Congress Control Number: 2004103899

Blue Note Publications
www.bluenotebooks.com
1-800-624-0401

Parents...   The story of Ikey originated as Sarah Becton watched her children gleefully chasing the little seashells as the waves washed them up out of the sand on the beach. The little coquina was always caught because he was very slow in tunneling himself back into the sand. The children always wanted to keep the little shells for pets. To help explain why they should not take the little shells out of their home in the sand, Sarah Becton would tell the children this story about Ikey, a little shell that was taken home from the beach by a little boy.

Ikey's story tells how Ikey was always exploring new things. Ikey's Uncle Ulee, had told many stories about the world beyond the ocean sand. Uncle Ulee had learned them from Ebert Seagull. Ikey felt that he had to do something to help himself see the big world. This world was full of dangers that Ikey never expected. Ikey heard sounds that terrified him. He learned what being hungry and sick was like. He had many adventures, but soon all he could think about was his nice safe home back with his family and friends.

As a reading and learning disability specialist, Sarah Becton used the story about Ikey's adventures to teach phonics skills to her classroom. They used the animal names as key words for the long vowel sounds. This story is also useful for parents who want to help their children learn the long vowel sounds.

Ikey was a little shell. He lived in the sand with his family. He did not like to be called by his real name, Isaac. So he had everyone call him Ikey.

Ikey lived with his mother and father, one brother, Abe, and one sister, Edith. They lived in a big shell down in the sand at the edge of the ocean.

7

Ikey's family lived next door to grandfather and grandmother Ohzee. The children liked to go by their house on the way home from school. Grandfather and grandmother Ohzee always gave them good things to eat.

Uncle and Aunt Ulee lived just around a big rock from where Ikey lived. Their house was the place to visit after dinner because Uncle Ulee always told good stories.

Ikey liked uncle Ulee's stories about the house where people lived. Uncle Ulee said the house had a lot of boxes. One box had music and pictures. Another box was full of fun things called toys.

13

Uncle Ulee had learned about people's houses from Ebert Seagull. He had met Ebert on the beach. Ebert told Uncle Ulee many stories about the places he had visited. Uncle Ulee would then share the stories with everyone.

15

Ikey said, "I wish I could fly like Ebert so I could visit new places."

Uncle Ulee just shook his head. "Ikey," he said, "you are a coquina like me. You have to learn to travel with your mind. It is hard to believe, but you are very lucky because you can't fly like Ebert. Without wings you will have to use your mind."

"I don't feel very lucky," said Ikey.

"I know," said Uncle Ulee, "listen to me. I will tell you how easy it is to travel with your mind. Just sit quietly, close your eyes, and breathe slowly and deeply into your stomach. With your eyes closed, look up toward your eyebrows and see yourself traveling. You could even visit the stars."

We are not all the same. We all have special looks that make us who we are. Ebert has wings and feathers that make him a bird. Your friend Obie has many arms that make him a starfish. You have a pretty shell that makes you a coquina. But you should not want to look or act like the others. Learn to be Ikey. Learn to be a good Ikey. So then, Ikey can like Ikey. Remember, "Ikey is Ikey's best friend."

21

The next day at school was not a good day for Ikey. This was because of Obie. Obie was a little starfish. He was Ikey's best friend part of the time. Obie had broken Ikey's best crayon. This had made Ikey very cross. The teacher had sent Ikey to the corner for shouting at Obie. Ikey blamed Obie for causing all the trouble.

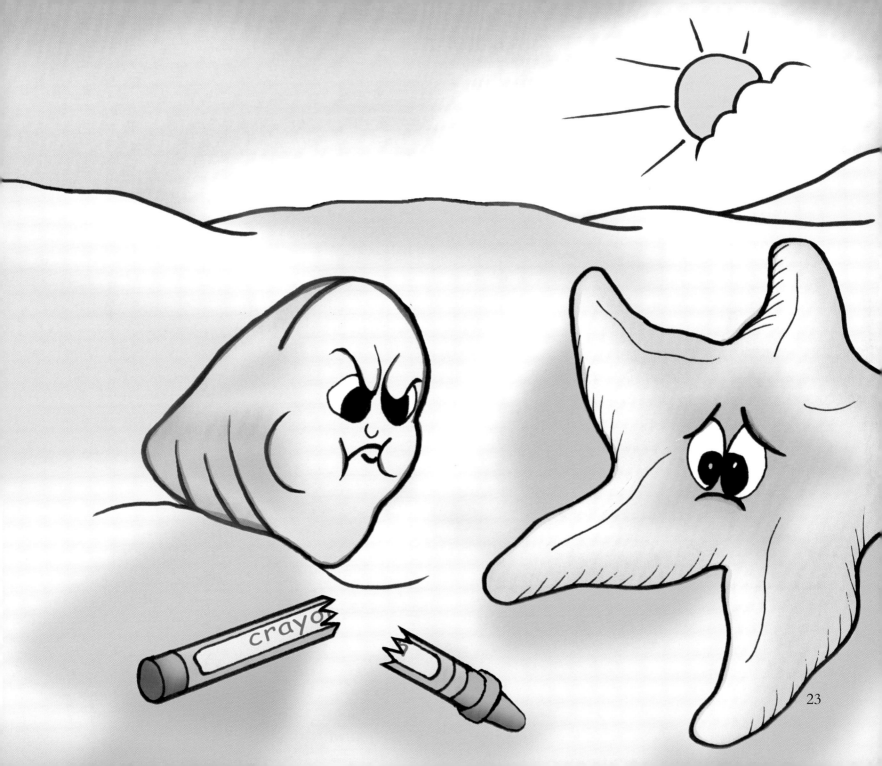

The teacher, nice Mrs. Abe, had said, "Ikey, now you have two nice crayons. You can share one crayon, and you will have one crayon to use."

Ikey didn't think it was fun to have short crayons. Everyone had short crayons. He had been so proud of his new long crayon, and now it was broken. This thought made him crosser than ever.

Ikey thought he would go find some of his friends and forget his bad day. His friends lived down in the sand close by him. Every day after school they played together. One of their best games was hiding in the rocks, and seaweed. But today Ikey would have to play by himself. He couldn't find anyone to play with him.

Ikey did not like it when the waves washed him up out of the sand and rocks. Sometimes the waves would turn him upside down. Today was a very bad day to turn Ikey upside down because he was very cross.

Ikey was not just cross. He was very sad about his bad day. He was bumped around by the waves, and up and down he went. He thought, "I just have to do something."

Ikey jumped as high as he could. He jumped on a big wave. Up, up he went to the top of the wave and off he sailed. "My what fun this is," thought Ikey, "I have never been on top of the waves before. Now here I am sailing along like a boat." Ikey had learned about boats in school.

Crash went Ikey as he hit the sand. He landed a long way from the water. This big crash showed Ikey one thing—all that goes up comes down.

"Wow!" said Ikey. "What is this by the side of me?" He was looking at ten little toes. Well, they were not very little to Ikey, but they were all in a row. "Let's see," said Ikey, "I'll just say hello." "Hello!" But he did not hear a thing. He watched and watched, but all they did was wiggle.

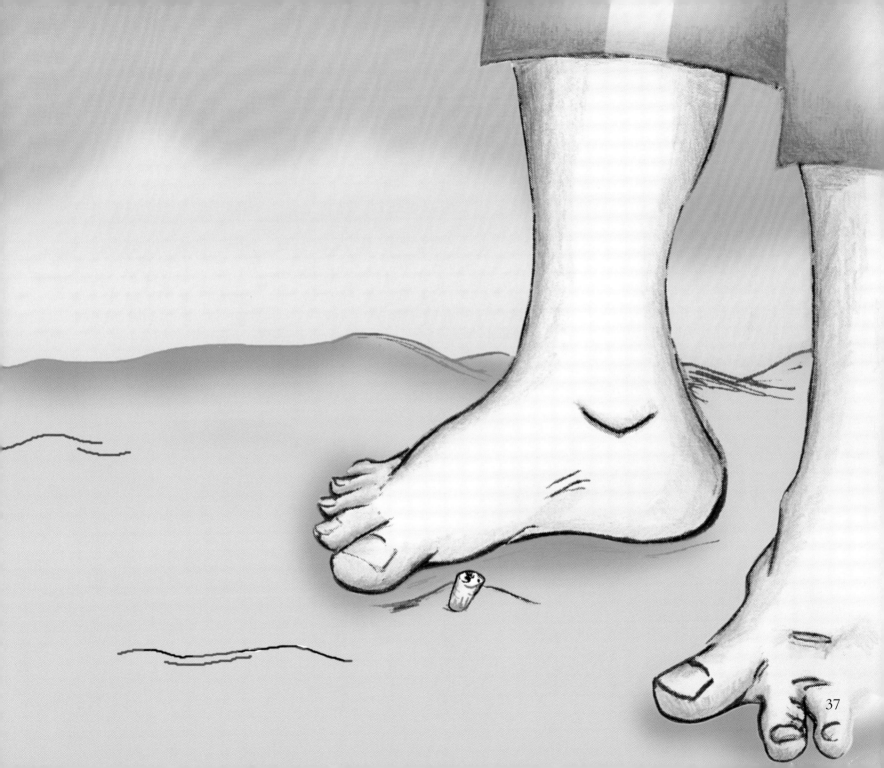

"This is funny," thought Ikey. "I will just climb up on top and see what is on the other side." So up, he went. "Well, there is no other side," said Ikey.

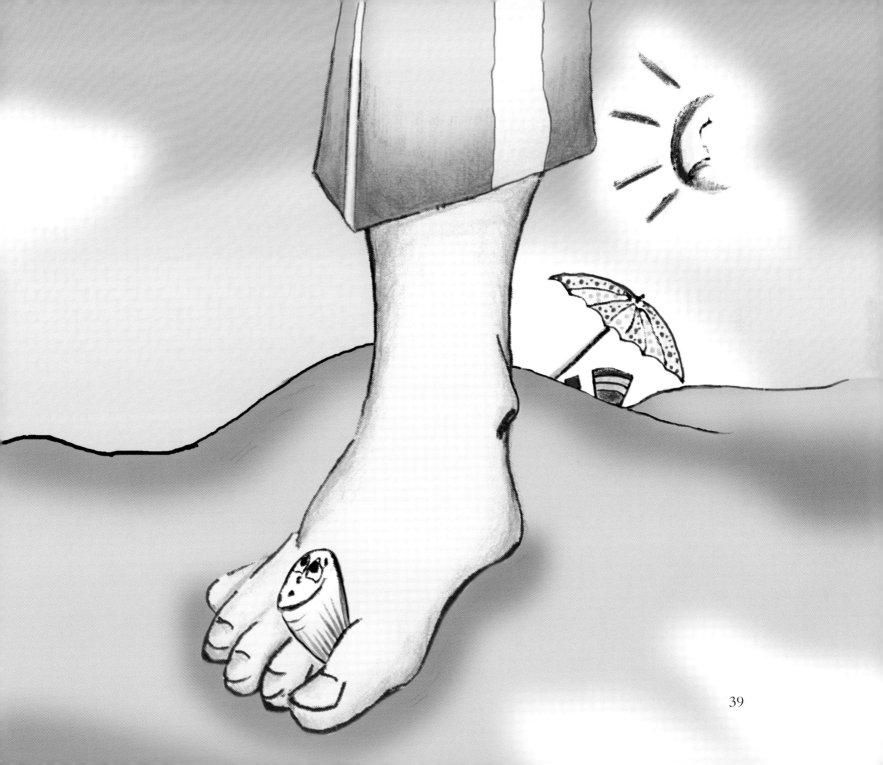

Just as Ikey made it to the top of the ten little things, they went swish, up and around. Ikey slipped into a very small space just in time to save himself from a big fall. He did not know why he was having such a rough ride. However, he was going up and down, flap, flap, on and on.

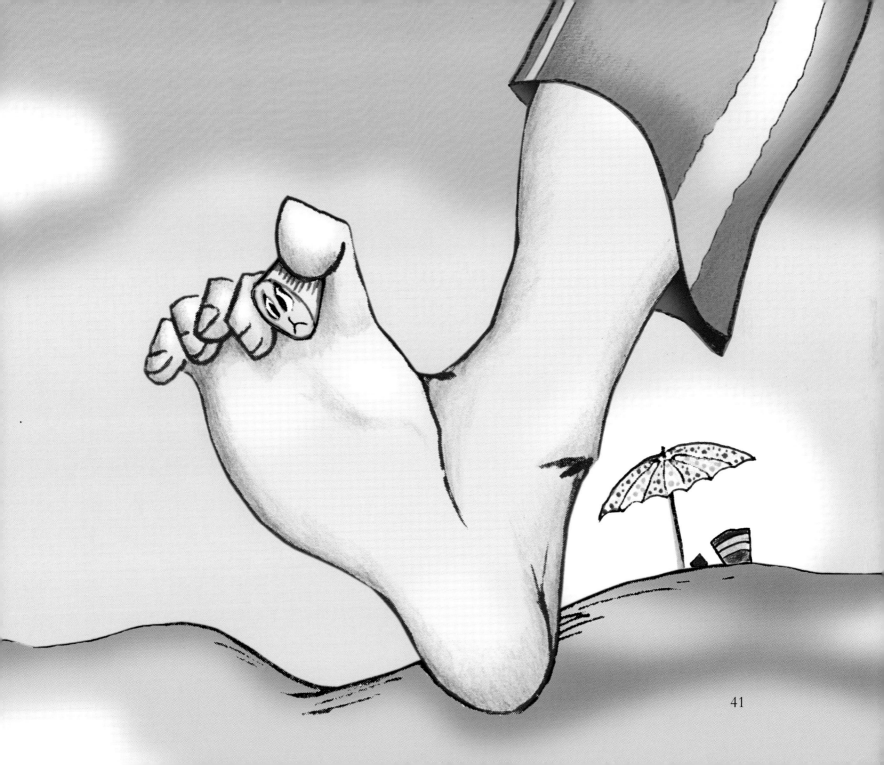

Ikey stopped moving at last. He looked around to see where he was. On top of the other side of the ten things – WOW – two big round things were looking right at him.

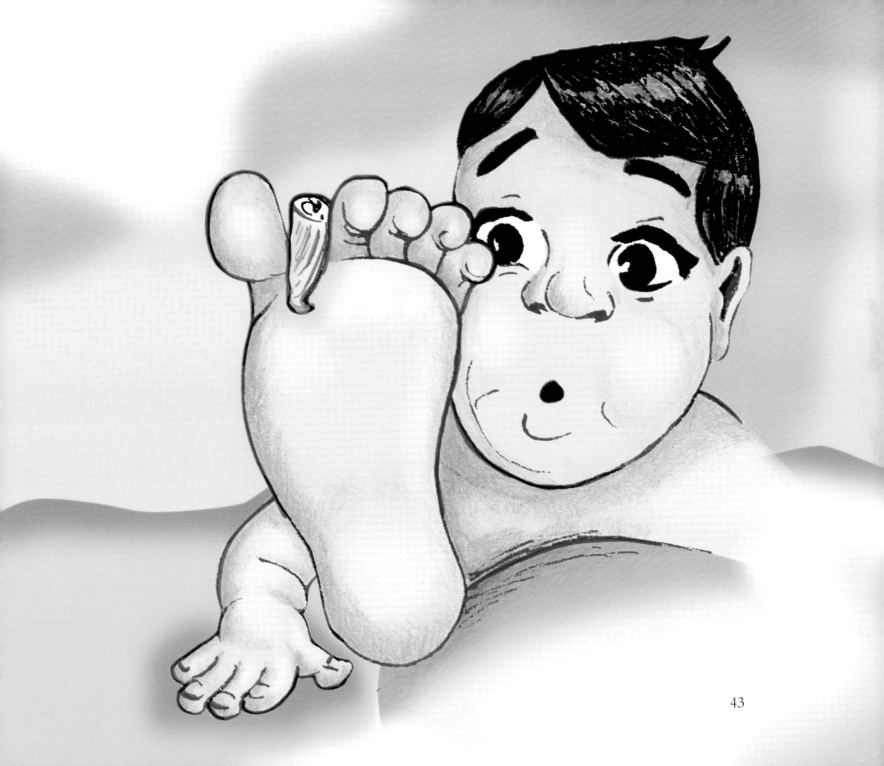

43

Ikey slipped back into his hiding place. He was trying to hide from the two things. Ikey did not know that the two eyes and ten toes belonged to a very good little boy. A little boy who loved all little things and wanted to take care of them.

45

The little boy helped Ikey out from his hiding place. He looked at Ikey with his two big eyes. However, Ikey was not afraid of his two big eyes anymore. He knew they would be friends. Ikey could tell from the nice soft way the little boy held him and talked to him.

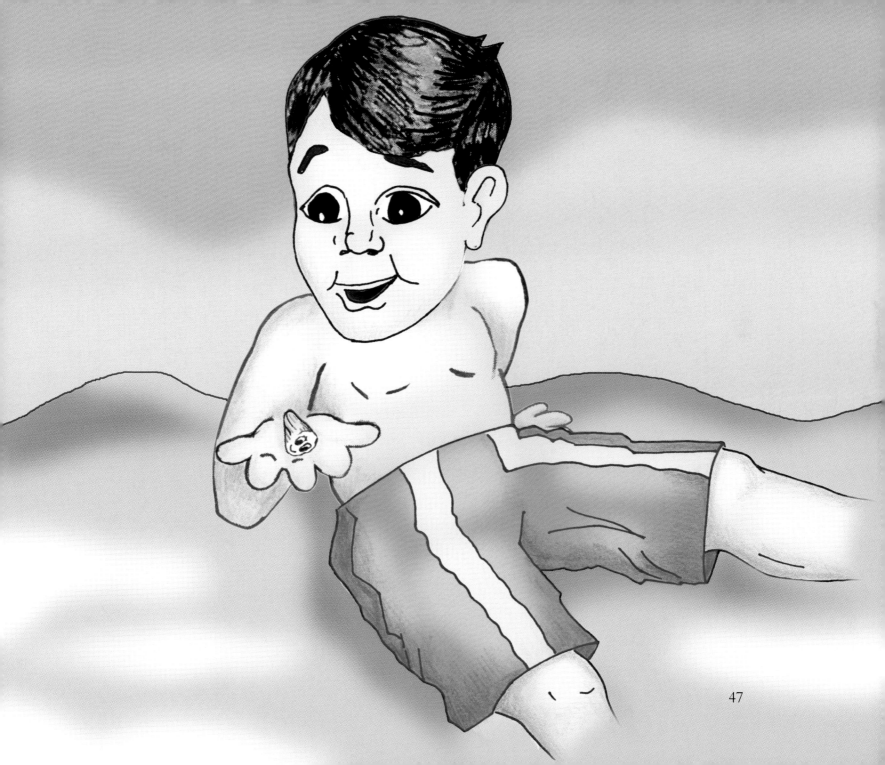

47

"Oh boy," thought Ikey, "maybe the little boy will take me home with him." Ikey was very happy thinking about all the nice things he had heard Uncle Ulee tell about little boys' houses. Maybe he could even watch the picture box.

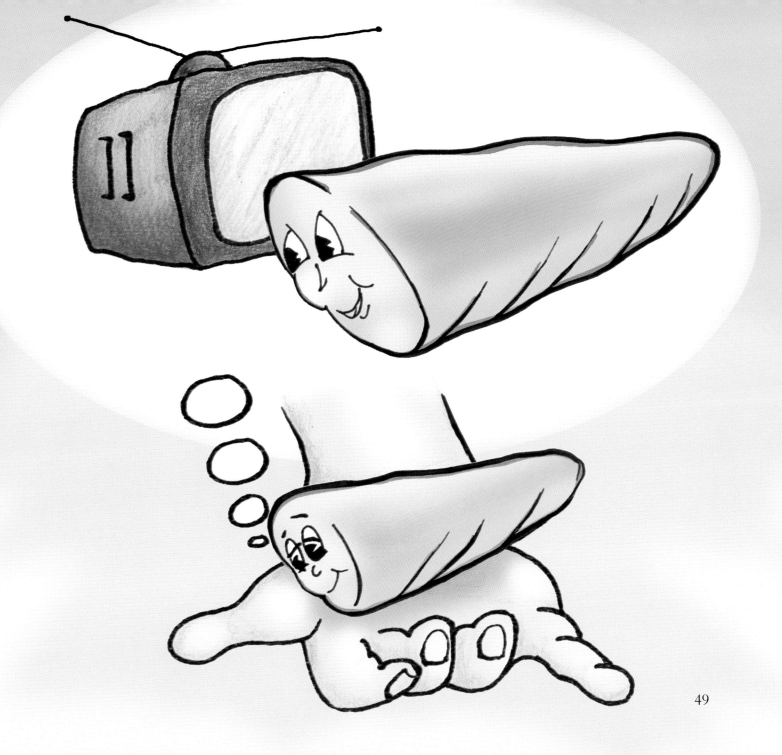

Just then he felt himself fall into something dark. It was a little like home. There was some sand and a frog in it. At first Ikey did not know where he was.

However, the little frog told him not to be afraid. After all, this was just the little boy's place for keeping all his best liked things. It was called a pocket. The little frog told Ikey his name was Gussy.

51

Gussy Frog and Ikey were bounced around in the dark little pocket. Suddenly the bouncing stopped. After they waited a little while, they decided to see what was on the outside. So up they went to the top of the pocket.

Just as Ikey had hoped, the little boy had taken them to his room. However, the room was not at all like Ikey had pictured it. What a mess! Old wet things were dumped in the middle of the floor.

Gussy Frog said, "The best place for us is back in the pocket!" So back they went into the pocket.

Ikey and Gussy Frog stayed in the pocket for a very long time. Gussy Frog told Ikey this happened to him all the time. Hearing this did not make Ikey feel very well. Now he was not so happy about being picked up.

57

Ikey wished for his home in the good, salty ocean. He missed his mother and father, sister and brother, and all his friends. He tried to think of all the things that they would be doing to find him. Maybe they would not even try to find him at all. This thought made him very sad.

59

He remembered Mrs. Abe, his teacher, and all his friends at school. He wished he had not been so cross with his best friend, Obie. Now that he thought about it, he was sure Obie had not meant to break his new crayon.

Poor Ikey didn't know that his family and all his friends were looking for him. Mrs. Abe, his teacher, had let all the children out of school to look for him. They were looking under the rocks and behind the seaweeds. Obie looked in all of Ikey's hiding places. They were all very unhappy because they could not find Ikey.

Grandfather Ohzee and Uncle Ulee tried to cheer everyone up by saying, "Ikey is all right. He will come back home safe and sound, you will see, you will see."

65

It seemed like days before they were picked up off the floor. At last, someone put them in a basket of wet things. They didn't smell very good, but at least they had been moved. Ikey and Gussy Frog thought they had better look to see where they were.

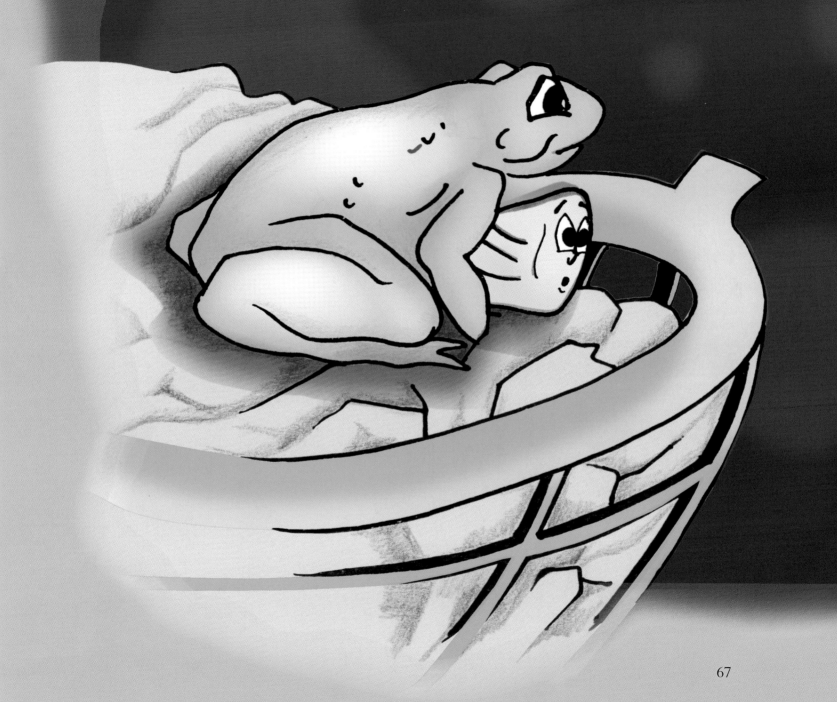

Just as Ikey and Gussy Frog came up out of the pocket, they saw a funny thing. It was big, white, and making a noise. Ikey didn't know what it was, but Gussy Frog knew. It was the boy's mother's wash day. He knew they had better jump, and jump now, before they landed in that big white thing.

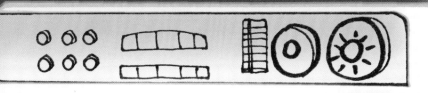

69

Just as Ikey and Gussy Frog started to jump, they saw two eyes looking at them. They were not the same two eyes Ikey had seen before.

Ikey did not know he was eye to eye with the little boy's mother. However, Gussy Frog knew mother. He had seen her before. Gussy Frog shoved Ikey back into the pocket and covered his own ears. It was just in time, too, because the blast Ikey heard made him think of a boat horn. However, this was only the way the little boy's mother acted when she saw Gussy Frog. Mother was not afraid of frogs. It was just that mother was not looking for frogs in her wash.

Gussy Frog told Ikey that mother would talk to the little boy. Then they would get a good place to live. Ikey said, "I hope you are right. I'm ready for a good place to live."

Gussy Frog was right. Ikey heard mother talking to the little boy. He did not know what she was saying to the little boy. However, Gussy Frog could understand mother. He told Ikey that mother was telling the little boy how they could fix a clean place for them to live, with fresh water and good food.

Mother told the little boy that a little frog and a little shell could not live in a little boy's pocket. She said a little frog eats flies and a little shell gets its food from the ocean water.

The little boy told mother that they could help the little frog catch flies. However, he did not know how to help the little shell. Mother got a bucket and said, "Come with me. I will show you." They went to the ocean and got Ikey some water to put in his new home.

The little boy fixed the picture box for Gussy Frog and Ikey to see. This made them very happy. He read them stories and showed them pictures. All that Ikey knew about a house was what Uncle Ulee had told him.

However, Gussy Frog knew all about it. He told Ikey about everything. He told him the picture box was called a TV. He also explained all the sounds in the house for Ikey.

Gussy Frog had learned to go under the water when he heard "mew-mew." Ikey did not think he would like "mew-mew," since Gussy Frog didn't.

83

When he heard "bow-wow," Ikey knew to look for big eyes, a funny nose, and a long tongue.

The little boy had many friends. They all liked to peep into Ikey and Gussy Frog's home. Sometimes the little boy's friends would pick up Ikey and Gussy. Ikey did not like this because they would poke him to get his feet out. Ikey kept his feet in because he knew it was safe inside the shell.

After many weeks, Gussy Frog told Ikey that mother wanted the little boy to take Ikey back to the ocean sand to live. Mother told the little boy that little animals like Ikey could not live out of the ocean. At first this news made the little boy sad. However, when he looked at Ike's sad little shell, he knew what mother was talking about. Ikey told Gussy Frog he would miss him. Gussy Frog said, "I'll come to visit you."

Next, the two friends said good-bye to each other. Then the little boy came and took Ikey back to the beach, just where he had found him. Mother had told the little boy that Ikey needed to find his mother and father. Ikey was so happy to be back home. For a few minutes he just lay and soaked up the good ocean water and felt the warm sand. Then he rushed home to see his family.

His mother and father and all the family were so happy to have him back. Grandfather Ohzee and Uncle Ulee just said over and over, "We knew he would come back home safe and sound, and here he is. We told you so, we told you so."

93

Mother hugged Ikey and said. "We are so glad to have you back. We missed you so much. How did you get lost?" Ikey said, "I'm sorry I caused so much trouble because I did what you told me not to do. I went up on top of the waves." Mother hugged Ikey again and said, "Ikey, I don't like what you did, but I will always love you."

About the Authors...

Sarah Walker Becton M.A.

Dr. Dan Becton

Sarah W. Becton retired after teaching for forty-four years. She has taught diagnostic and corrective reading and exceptional student education for handicapped children in addition to classroom teaching. She earned her Bachelors Degree at Middle Tennessee State University and taught in public schools in Tennessee. Her first three years she taught with Ruth Bowdoin, the author of the famous Bowdoin program. Ruth Bowdoin continues to be a major influence on her work. Mrs. Becton completed her Master's degree in the Art of Teaching from Rollins College, Florida. In addition to reading Certification, she is certified in Early Childhood, Varying Exceptionalities and Learning Disabilities.

This is the first in a series of six books she wrote to tutor beginning readers. She has lived at the beach in Indialantic for over forty years so the little beach creature was a natural for her first work. Ikey incorporates characters featuring all the long vowel sounds.

Dr. Dan Becton is the Director of Exceptional Student Educati for Clay County Schools near Jacksonville in Green Cove Sprin Florida. He has taught in classes for students with Learning Disabil at the elementary and junior high school levels. His Bachelors Deg is from Vanderbilt University and his Masters Degree in Specia Education is from the University of New Mexico. His Ph.D. degr is from the University of Florida in Educational Psychology. He l done artwork for many years and did both artwork and photogra when in the U.S. Navy. He is also an adjunct instructor for the University of North Florida and Nova Southeastern University.